The Toll Road

3 stories

Kristina Turnage

Wandering in the Words Press

For permission, visit
www.wanderinginthewordspress.com

All characters in this book are fictitious, and any resemblance to real persons, living or dead, is coincidental.

PUBLISHED BY WANDERING IN THE
WORDS PRESS

ISBN-10: 0-9976355-2-5
ISBN-13: 978-0-9976355-2-2

First Edition

To my husband, Joe, for always encouraging me.
And to my parents, for letting me follow my dream.

TABLE OF CONTENTS

THE TOLL ROAD

The pain slashed across my cheek, lighting a fire under my skin, but I realized only a second later that the pain of a fist was nothing when my head was forcibly slammed into the ground by the heel of a boot. For a few seconds I slipped in and out of consciousness, a temporary relief that was over as quickly as it began. The asphalt road was cold and unforgiving beneath my face. More feet made contact with my ribs and stomach, but a voice called out, and the beating ceased. My ears rang, and I could feel something wet on my cheek. I touched my face and felt the blood trickling from my split lip. I tried to sit up, but a boot connected with my stomach again, and all the air went from my lungs. Coughing, I threw my arms out to protect my face.

I had never been in a fight before, not in school growing up or later when I was in college. It wasn't that I had gone out of my way to avoid being in fights. I wasn't a self-proclaimed hippie, spouting peace and harmony crap. I had always been the nice guy, the guy who would give you a ride home if you'd had one too many drinks, or even the guy who passed up the opportunity to make out with an inebriated—and gorgeous—Carly Matheson because I was still seeing Emily Sutton. If anything, I was too nice, but things were different now. The world had become unrecognizable almost overnight, and it was a rough place for a nice guy like me.

"Hey, you should have just paid the toll, *amigo*," said a voice nearby just as another fist made contact with my jaw. It was the same voice that had called out, and I realized that the voice had been speaking Spanish. My heartbeat roared in my ears.

I never should have been with them. I never should have trusted anyone. How can you trust when the world has been plunged into chaos? *Stay calm*, the police had said, but that was seven weeks ago. No one was calm anymore.

"I'm sorry," I tried to say, but the words sounded jumbled.

The leader of the gang leaned down until his face was inches from my own. He was Hispanic or Latino. I couldn't tell. His head was shaved, the corner of a tattoo just visible on the side of his neck. A bandana covered the bottom of his face, and for just a moment I forgot that this was really happening and thought maybe I had walked onto a film set or something. Do gangs really wear bandanas like that? I had never seen a real gang before. But then I remembered the car, the torches on either side of the road, and the men standing in the way.

It had all happened so fast. Jesse and his brother Eric had been in the front seat of the old Buick they had stolen some time before I'd met them. They had promised me that I would be in North Carolina by the next day at least, but that was before they picked up the homeless guy. Technically we were all homeless now, but this guy had been homeless for years, long enough that his skin looked like leather and several of his teeth were missing. I could still smell him, a stench so strong that it hung around him like a cloud. I told the brothers that we should leave the guy. We didn't need to give him a ride; someone else could help him. They hadn't been able to resist the whiskey bottle that the homeless guy had flashed at us as payment for the lift. I should have gotten out of the car right then.

"We don't want to have to kill you, too," the gang leader said slowly so that I would understand his meaning.

The torch lit up a pair of feet several yards away. They looked like Eric's shoes, grey sneakers that had once been white and new. I waited for them to move, twitch, anything, but they lay perfectly still. A black puddle slowly spread out around them.

I remembered how Jesse had stopped the car when the lights had come into view. We had seen about eight men standing in the road. It looked like one of them had a bat in his hands. Jesse and Eric exchanged worried glances, but the homeless guy took a swig from the whiskey bottle and handed it to Jesse.

"What in the hell should we do?" Eric asked.

"Shit," the homeless guy said, his voice slurred. "Run 'em down."

I tried to laugh it off. Of course we weren't going to run down a bunch of men—because people just don't do that, not even now in this broken world.

"We'll find another way through," I said, but it had no effect.

Jesse took one long swig off the whiskey bottle before slamming his foot down on the gas pedal and screaming maniacally. Beside me in the backseat, the homeless guy's eyes had gone wild. I think I was screaming for them to stop when the truck slammed into the side of the car.

Now, as the gang leader watched me, waiting for me to react to Eric's lifeless body, I wished that there had been something I could have done to stop all this. I went over the scene in my head again and again, looking for my missed opportunity. The gang leader looked from me to Eric to the destroyed truck.

"Where y'all going in such a hurry, *amigo?* You couldn't even stop to ask us to let you pass? Now that is just rude." He looked to the man beside him, a burly guy with meaty arms. "Alex, can you believe this? This guy was going to kill us. We had to ruin the front of a perfectly good truck to keep him from killing us all."

"No!" I managed to shout. "I told them to stop."

My nose was definitely broken, but now that they had stopped hitting me, my head wasn't as fuzzy. I tried to get my bearings. There were nearly a dozen of them, though I couldn't be certain; woods on either side of the highway, could easily obscure a larger group. I sat up slowly, keeping my hands visible by my sides.

***

At first it had been the noise, the god-awful noise. Explosions and screams had filled my ears. I had run to my bathroom, closed the door, and buried my face in a towel. I stayed in there for over an hour, until finally I had convinced myself that nothing about the tiny room was any safer than the rest of my apartment.

The power had gone out a few seconds after I had locked the bathroom door, but I hoped my cell phone would help shed some light on whatever was happening. I found it on the desk in my living room, still buried underneath the essays I'd been grading. Still on, but no service; the battery was almost dead, too.

Stay calm.

I had an old radio in the back of my closet. I dug it out, popped in some batteries, and turned it on. When I turned the dial, though, there was nothing. A complete blackout. My heart raced. Outside, it was all commotion. Sirens filled the air, and all around my apartment building I heard voices. Taking a deep breath to steady my nerves, I walked to the window so that I could see for myself what was happening.

Ribbons of green light undulated in the evening sky, a sight I had seen only in pictures of Alaska. Off in the distance, the Dallas skyline was dark, and it reminded me that I was a long ways from Alaska and the Northern Lights.

Unless.

A terrible thought crossed my mind. There had been a story on the news a few years ago, about how sometimes, if the conditions were right, the Northern Lights could be seen much farther south.

Solar flare.

The words jumped around inside my head. I found a flashlight in my kitchen and went to the bookcase by my desk. On the bottom shelf was an old encyclopedia that I hadn't touched in years, a gift from my grandparents when I'd graduated from high school. I found the volume labeled *S* and flipped until I located the entry. It was really just a definition, none of which made much sense to me, but at the bottom of the entry it read: *see coronal mass ejection.* I put the volume back and grabbed the *C* volume, found the right page, and then quickly wished that I hadn't bothered to look it up. I wasn't really sure what a geomagnetic storm was, but it didn't sound good. I went back to my window with the book clutched in my hands and wondered if my sister was safe.

***

"What is your name, *amigo?*"

A bottle of water was shoved into my hand. I took it warily but couldn't bring myself to drink from it. The leader of the gang saw my hesitancy and scowled. He snatched the bottle and took a swig from it before thrusting it back at me. An intense feeling of shame coursed through me. I took a sip.

"I'm sorry. I didn't used to be like this," I said, my voice raspy. It felt as though I had swallowed gravel. I took another sip of water and then another. "My name is Jake. Jake Sheffield."

"How long were you with your buddies there?" he asked, motioning with his head toward the car. The gang leader snatched the bottle back from my hands and passed it to one of his men.

"Not long, only a couple of days. I needed a ride. They gave me one. What do I call you?"

It was the first question that I had asked, and it seemed a harmless one. I was under no delusions that just because I was still alive meant that I would stay that way. It would only take one word from him, and one of his guys would bash in my head. He may even kill me himself.

"You can call me Lopez," he said with a shrug. I assumed that was his last name, but I didn't want to ask. He said something in Spanish to his group.

Two of the gang members built a fire nearby. They stacked branches like a teepee and stuffed leaves around it. Flames quickly climbed up the branches and warded off the oppressive darkness. Lopez and I sat near the edge of the circle so that when I looked at him he was still in the shadows, his face difficult to read.

"What are you going to do with me?" I asked, unable to bear the suspense any longer.

"I am still figuring that out," he said. "We do not like to hurt people. I know what you're thinking,

Jake, but really we are not all so bad. In these times, though, you have to protect what is yours. You see, Jake, just down this road there is a small town. When the green lights came, and all this shit began, many people came through our town, and not all of them were nice."

He moved into the light for the first time so that I could see him more clearly. He pulled the bandana from his face and used it to wipe the sweat from his brow. Lopez was older than I had realized, closer to my own age, perhaps in his late twenties or early thirties. He looked at me with an intensity and calmness that I hadn't expected. There was no cruelty there, no sign of meanness. He shoved the bandana into his jacket pocket. He patted his pants until he found a crumpled pack of cigarettes. He pulled one out and let it dangle from his lips while he searched in his jacket for a lighter. He found one and sat smoking in silence. I watched this ritual, not wanting to speak unless I had to. Finally, he exhaled loudly, a stream of smoke billowing out into the night air.

"I have a family in that town, Jake. My wife, my daughter, they live in that town. We all have a family there," he said, pointing to the other men. They were all listening to him, waiting along with me to find out what my fate would be. "I am not going to let harm come to that town. It's why we watch the road. Now I am going to ask you a very important question, Jake, and your answer had better sound like the truth to me."

He leaned forward and took a drag of his cigarette, the smoke streaming out his mouth a moment later. Fear filled my entire body, pulsed through my veins. Would he believe anything I said, even if what I said was the absolute truth?

"Why should I let you pass through my town where you could hurt my family? Why should I trust you?"

I realized in that moment that I was the enemy here, not them. To them I was the unknown threat to their families. If I had a wife and child, would I also take up arms with my neighbors to protect them? I had never been a violent person, but then these were unusual times—when any man could be dangerous. Everyone has their own definition of survival.

"I have a sister," I said. "Sarah lives in North Carolina, and I don't even know if she's okay."

"Is that why you took a ride from those guys?"

"Yes. They said they were going to Virginia. They were going to pass right through North Carolina, so they let me ride along with them. Then they picked up the homeless guy, even though I told them not to. I ... I should have left when they picked him up, but I didn't. I just want to get to Sarah."

***

"You should come visit this Christmas. I haven't seen you in nearly two years."

"I'll try, but I can't make any promises," I had told her as I pulled a stack of papers from my briefcase.

I listened to her as she complained about how rarely we saw each other. My brother-in-law, Dave, had been deployed to the Middle East for four months, and my nephew was becoming more difficult.

"It would do us both some good if you came to visit. Brian needs his uncle right now."

"Sarah, I wish I could see you more. You know that." I didn't want to upset her, but she tended to forget that teachers don't make a lot of money. If I flew to North Carolina every time she asked me to, I'd be broke.

"Listen, I'll call you later, and we'll talk about this some more. I have to get these papers graded or else my students are going to think I'm torturing them. Okay?"

"Fine," she said. The call started to break up so that I didn't hear the last thing she said, but it sounded like "I love you."

"I love you, too, Sarah."

I put the phone down and reached for my briefcase again. I paused to run my hand over the leather. My father's initials were embossed in one corner. I had once thought that I would teach college like he had, but in the end I had settled for a position at a small private high school. The students were all overachievers, too eager to grow up. Had he lived long enough to see me graduate from college, I know my father would have been proud that I was teaching, but I always wondered what it would be like to have a different career. I had imagined myself with a corner office, a sports car, and an expense account. I saw guys like that often enough when I went out with friends in the city—Dallas was full of them—but when I walked into my classroom every day and saw the students' faces staring at me, eager to learn, I understood why my father loved it so much. It's the only time I ever felt connected to him.

***

My hands were bound tightly in my lap with rope. The flames cast shadows on the woods, and I half expected to see faces staring out at me from the depths of the forest, floating ghost-like between the tree trunks. As far as I could tell, Lopez had been telling the truth when he said they were only there to protect the town that lay farther down the road.

Lopez carried a torch to the car, illuminating the crumpled metal. The truck had caved in the driver's side, and inside the car, broken and bloody, Jesse's body slumped over the steering wheel. Lopez walked around to the other side of the vehicle. The door hung open from when they had pulled me out. I wondered where the homeless man's body was or if he was still alive. I felt terrible for thinking it, but I hoped that they wouldn't tie him up beside me.

Lopez pulled something from the car, but I couldn't see what it was. He went back and pulled something else out. I caught a glimpse of my briefcase. For the first time since everything had gone bad I wanted to cry. Lopez threw my briefcase on the ground and went back to the car again. He stripped it of all the food and water we had packed. When he was done, he motioned to the others to finish the job and walked back to me.

"Is one of those bags yours?" he asked.

I tried to keep my voice calm and steady, but it broke when I told him that the briefcase was mine. "There's not much inside. Just a change of clothes, some water, and a few packs of trail mix."

He went to the pile and picked it up. He brought it back and set it down next to me. My hands itched to run over the leather, to feel the initials under my fingers. I had been very careful when I packed, taking only the basic essentials, but when I had to choose between a practical duffel bag and my briefcase, I had been unable to leave the briefcase behind. I had tucked pictures of my family, a copy of my favorite Hemingway novel, and—just in case— my cell phone into the pockets. I had packed more food, but when I teamed up with Jesse and Eric, we had pooled all our rations together. I had kept only what I might need if I got separated from them.

Lopez tried to open it, but it was locked. He fumbled with the built-in combination. He pulled a pocket knife from his pants and worked at it. I expected the lock to break and was just as surprised as he was when it held. I couldn't help the feeling of pride that welled up inside of me.

"Are you going to tell me the combination?"

"Why?"

"I just want to make sure there are no weapons in here. I have to protect my friends. You know that, Jake. So tell me the combination."

I touched my tongue to my lip, felt where it was split. My nose throbbed worse than my ribcage. I looked Lopez in the eyes. The man was no fool, and neither was I.

"Five. Nine. Seven."

He turned the dials, the lock clicked, and the two clasps sprang open. He pulled everything out of the briefcase one item at a time and set the two water bottles and the packs of trail mix off to the side. He flipped through the pages of the book and scanned the faces in the photographs before tossing them on top of the novel. Sarah's smiling face looked up at me as Lopez unfolded my shirt and pants. My cell phone fell out, but he retrieved it and tossed it onto my pile of belongings. When he was satisfied that there was nothing else of importance inside, he threw the briefcase to the ground.

"Are you going to kill me?" I asked, unable to stand the silence any longer.

He sat down beside me and rested his arms on his legs; his face remained hidden in the shadows. If he was going to kill me, I wished that he would go ahead and get it over with. I hoped it would be quick—that Lopez wouldn't make me suffer.

"Is your sister alone?"

"She has a son, my nephew. His name is Brian. He's only six. Her husband is a Marine."

"So she has someone to take care of her then."

"No!" I realized a moment too late that Lopez was searching for a reason to let me live, a good reason. "Dave's deployed. His unit had been deployed to the Middle East for five months when it happened. He should have come home by now, but then everything happened. I don't know if he's with her. I don't know! I have to make sure she's okay."

Tears ran down my cheeks. I wiped my face on my sleeve. There was nothing left now. I had given Lopez everything. He knew who I was, where I was from. He had seen the only possessions that I had left in the world. There was nothing left to give him.

He said something in Spanish to Alex. Alex nodded. He pulled a bandana from his back pocket and walked toward me.

"Lopez, please. You have to believe me. I would never harm you or anyone else," I said.

Alex came up behind me and tied the bandana around my head, covering my eyes. I struggled against the rope that held my hands together until it felt like my wrists would break. Suddenly I was being lifted into the air. I kicked out at the arms holding my feet, but they were strong arms. They set me down on a cold, hard surface, and a moment later, when I heard and felt the engine roar to life, I realized that I was in the back of the truck. It coughed and sputtered, damaged from slamming into our car I supposed, but then we rumbled down the road. We sped up, faster and faster. Then we turned left, and then right. Soon we had turned so many times that I could no longer tell which direction we had come from. That was the point. We drove for what felt like miles and miles, but I don't think that more than fifteen minutes had gone by when suddenly we came to a stop.

The truck doors opened, and then hands grabbed my legs and pulled me. The bandana was yanked from my head. The two men who had built the fire stood before me. One held a bat in his hands, the other a knife. There was a ringing in my ears. Lopez stood behind them, watching. I closed my eyes, almost wishing that I were still blindfolded, and then I felt the knife slip between my wrists and the rope fall away. I looked up, relief washing over me.

"People are dangerous, Jake," Lopez said. It sounded both like a warning and advice. I took it as both. "Go find your sister, *amigo.*"

The man with the bat went to the truck, and when he came back, he shoved my briefcase into my arms. I held onto it like a life raft. It wasn't empty, that much I could tell, but whether or not they had left me any food or water I wasn't sure. I jumped down from the bed of the truck and wobbled on my feet. I took a painful step, and then another; it felt as though all my bones were broken. I kept my back to them, praying that this wasn't a trick, but I heard the truck doors close and then the engine start. I put one foot in front of the other, my eyes trained on the road ahead. Behind me, the truck turned around and sped off, the puttering of the muffler soon faint. After I had walked for nearly an hour, I stopped and ran my hand over the initials. I set the case down and opened it. My clothes, the book, the pictures, even my water and trail mix—it was all there. I pulled everything out and folded my pants. When I picked up my shirt, something fell to the ground. I picked it up with stunned disbelief. It was a knife, about six inches long, the hilt wrapped in black tape. It felt good in my palm. I looked down the road behind me, where there was no sign of the truck or a town. Then I turned my feet eastward and kept on walking.

REVOLUTION

The crowd cheers as a diploma is handed to the girl in front of me, and then I hear my own name called out through the loud speaker: "Laura Elizabeth Haywood." No one cheers. In fact, the silence is almost deafening as everyone watches me cross the stage and accept my diploma. I am not the only one suffering this treatment today. Other Strays are graduating, as well.

I shake the university president's hand and smile a fake smile for the camera, though I know no one is going to want that picture, especially me. I cross to the other side of the stage back toward my seat, ignoring the armed guards in white who watch my every move. The crowd cheers again as the next name is called. It's nothing new to me, this behavior, and so many others just like me have to endure the cold looks of distrust and hatred. I am one of the Strays, a child of the last regime. We are a constant reminder to those wanting to rebel that they will be killed, and that loyalists will raise their children. I think that in the beginning, His Highest was hoping that he would create a new generation of citizens loyal to the Domitus regime, but our Guardians—those who were supposed to be most loyal—often had trouble accepting us as their own children. Instead, they treated us like pariahs.

As soon as the ceremony is over, I leave. I'm ready to be home, away from the staring eyes and the whispers. Rain pummels me when I head outside, and I'm happy to see that the city electro-bus is coming down the street. The driverless bus hums to a stop at the corner. I climb the steps and swipe my pay card on the passenger scanner. I quickly do the math in my head and realize that if I am not careful I will not have enough money to go grocery shopping. My allowance is not enough to pay for luxuries.

I take a seat and turn to the window, away from the other people on the bus. I watch the rain running in rivulets down the window, enjoying the way it distorts the black buildings rushing past. I'm saddened that the city hardly has any trees. At least their leaves would provide some color and a distraction from the monotony. Aside from a few green patches in the parks that dot the landscape, the town is black. As a Stray, I am not allowed to leave the city and go to where there are still trees and rivers, where the ruins of the old country are grown over with vines. I once went on a school trip to see the ruins and learn about the country called America. My teacher told us that His Highest had pulled us up out of the ashes of the old country.

The man sitting beside me on the bus coughs, startling me. He glances in my direction, quickly dismisses me, and goes back to his newspaper. I take in his white suit and large briefcase. The fabric is of a fine quality, and his briefcase is made of real leather. He's probably a business owner or maybe a solicitor. I notice a brown stain on his knee. The sight of it reassures me for some reason, this small imperfection. He sees me staring at the stain, which looks like coffee, and tries to hide it with his hand. I look away, trying hard not to smile. The woman on the other side of the bus gives me a reproachful look, so I resume my gazing out of the bus window.

The electro-bus makes several stops before finally reaching my corner. The rain has stopped, and I take my time walking along the sidewalk, enjoying the momentary break in the weather. My neighborhood, which consists of only two apartment buildings near the edge of the city, is quiet. People come and go here so quickly that I rarely get to make friends. I'm left alone, which is better than being constantly harassed. My neighbors smile at each other in the hallway, help each other when they can, and make small talk when there's time, but we all know that it won't be long before someone comes into one of our apartments in the middle of the night and takes us away somewhere. I live in a last-chance building for those who speak out against the government. I'm the only one who stays here longer than a year, but this rundown building is all that my allowance can pay for if I want to be able to eat.

I take the stairs two at a time, smiling at the little girl playing with her dolls on the second-floor landing, and head up to the third floor. My apartment is small and barren—blue furniture in a white room. A red light turns on in the watcher box over my door. I head toward the refrigerator, hoping to find something to eat, but the phone rings before I get there. I press the button on the small screen in the wall, and my neighbor's face appears.

"Laura, sweetie, I just heard you come home. Are you hungry? I just made dinner for Bob and myself, but he's not here anymore," she says in a shaky voice.

Her eyes are red and puffy. For a second, I'm confused, until I realize what she's just said. I nod my head and she hangs up, the screen going black. Mrs. Litz and her husband moved in last month after her husband was overheard at work complaining about pay grades and taxes. Out of all the neighbors, I like the Litzes the best and have become friends with them, though I normally avoid doing that. How could I not when they practically invited themselves over the moment they'd moved in, but it was nice having two people who were actually happy to see me every day.

Across the hall, Mrs. Litz opens her door at my knock. She looks like she's been crying. The smell of dinner cooking fills the small apartment and makes my mouth water instantly. I realize I haven't eaten today. Her apartment is identical to mine—the same white walls, the same blue furniture. The only difference is that our apartments are mirror images of each other, down to the placement of the kitchen windows and the small fireplaces, which are our only sources of heat in the winter.

"Mrs. Litz, are you sure? Maybe there's been a mistake?" I ask.

She pushes me into a kitchen chair. She doesn't have to tell me what happened. "No, I'm certain. They left a notice on my door this morning. I knew this would happen. Her voice breaks as she ladles potato and leek soup into a bowl. She pauses for a moment, collecting herself, before bringing me the dish. She sits down at the table, and I reach across for her hand.

"I'm really sorry, Mrs. Litz." I don't say anything else because there really isn't anything I can say. He won't be coming back. We both know that. They never come back, and we are both wondering how long it will be before they come for her, even though she hasn't done anything wrong. They always take the rest of the family away.

"You should spend more time with some of the other Strays." She watches me while I eat. "It would be good for you to have some friends, someone you can talk to."

"You know I can't do that, Mrs. Litz. He'll wonder why we suddenly want to be friends. He'll think we're planning something. Besides, what would we have to talk about? How miserable our lives are? No, thank you."

I can see her wanting to argue with me, but she doesn't. Instead, she takes my dishes to the sink and wipes the counters down.

"I'm really glad that I got to meet you, Laura," she says unexpectedly. "You're a very sweet girl, despite what they say. And I'm proud of you for finishing school, even though I know how you feel about it. I want you to know that I'll miss you."

"Don't say this stuff. That's what will get you sent away, Mrs. Litz. I'm sure if you're very good, then they'll leave you alone."

She clucks at me, but I see her glance quickly at the watcher box over the door.

I promise Mrs. Litz that I'll come over for lunch the next day, and head back to my own apartment. I lean back against the door and close my eyes. I knew it would happen one day. I never doubted it, but I'm still shocked at how quickly it happened. Bob Litz was a truly nice man, but he had a tendency to say whatever was on his mind, no matter who was listening. When they moved in, Bob had offered to help me around the apartment. He took out my garbage and fixed a broken cabinet. It was like having a dad.

***

Early morning sunshine pours through my bedroom window, spilling across my bed. I've been awake for hours, watching the sunrise, waiting for a reason to get out of bed.

I feel strange knowing that I have nothing to do today except have lunch with Mrs. Litz. I've been going to school for as long as I can remember. My career was assigned when I was a young child, just like it was for the rest of us. Most Strays end up with menial jobs, but I was lucky to be given a teaching position. I'm beginning to dread it, though. The strict and structured lesson plans haven't changed in years, and I loathe the idea of repeating the same ideas to the next generation of impressionable minds.

My mind wanders to my upcoming birthday and what I know will happen. Every year His Highest comes to see me on my birthday. The Wexfords, my Guardians, loved his visits, but they were also a constant reminder to them that I was not their child. They could never love me. They never even pretended that they did, but they let me stay until I turned eighteen. Of course, they made sure I was gone the day after my eighteenth birthday.

"I'm just tired of having to take care of a Stray. You're nothing but a burden, Laura," Mrs. Wexford had said that morning. She had fixed me breakfast as usual and then had proceeded to tell me that it would no longer be necessary for me to live under their roof.

I was mortified having to contact His Highest to tell him that I would not be living in my Guardians' home. He made the arrangements for me to receive an allowance, helped me find my apartment, and for a while, I tried to delude myself into thinking he was being kind. Now I'm not so naïve.

My nerves twist tighter and tighter, and I feel like I might have a panic attack. I hate seeing His Highest—with his charcoal gray suit and perfectly sculpted hair—sitting in my living room, violating my space. I have to get out of bed. I can't lie here anymore. I take a shower, hoping the water will calm me down. After twenty minutes, I realize that it's not working, and I get out. I grab a towel, wipe the fog from the mirror, and run a comb through my wet hair. Dark circles rim my eyes. I've lost weight over the last few weeks. The skin is tighter over my cheekbones, making them appear sharper, but that normally happens around this time of the year. I sigh. There is just no hope for today. I grab a shirt and some pants—all white in accordance with the law—and pull my hair back. I grab my keys and head out the door to check my message box.

I see it as soon as I enter the hallway. The notice is tacked on the door, red and impenetrable, and it stops me in my tracks. I knew it would happen, but I hadn't thought that it would be so soon.

Due to heinous acts against His Highest, the residents herein have been removed for your safety.

"No," I say before I can stop myself. I quickly glance up and down the hallway, paranoia spiking wildly, but I'm alone, so I doubt that anyone heard me. I keep walking toward the stairwell, my heart pounding in my chest, and go down to the first floor. My hands shake as I lift the lid on my message box. My fingers find one small envelope inside, thin and unassuming, until I realize who sent it. I hurriedly tuck it into my pocket, not ready to open it yet.

I walk to the coffee shop at the end of the street and pass another Stray, John Wolfe. He smiles at me, but I look away, not glancing back at him until I open the door to the coffee shop. I think about what Mrs. Litz had said about being friends with the other Strays, but I can't bring myself to call out to him, to invite him for coffee. Instead I go inside, letting the door swing shut behind me.

The owner is behind the counter today. I give him my order and try not to stare at the long scar that runs down the left side of his face. I have seen it many times before, and I always wonder how he got it. Was it an accident with a really great story to go with the scar or, more likely, a punishment rendered in the beginning of His Highest's reign? I'm too afraid to ask, and I doubt that he would ever tell me anyway. He hands me the hot paper cup, and I hand him my pay card. He swipes it and hands it back to me without even making an effort to smile. I slip the card back into my pocket and leave the coffee shop.

I find a bench just on the edge of one of the small community parks—though the word "park" is hardly fitting since there are no trees here, only grass—and sit down. I set my coffee beside me and pull out the letter. The handwriting on the envelope is ornate, the thick black ink curling over the paper. I turn it over, slide my finger under the flap, and carefully tear it open. There is only a single sheet of parchment paper, cream-colored and expensive. The letter is written with the same ink, in the same hand—his secretary's handwriting. I read the letter carefully and then reread it as I try to understand what it means.

It seems that His Highest is not coming to visit me; instead, this year I will go to him in The Tower. I can't help glancing up at the massive building of tinted windows and black steel. I feel as if he is up there looking down at me, and a shiver runs down my spine, despite the heat of the afternoon. I put the letter back in its envelope.

***

I try to go to bed early, but I keep dreaming about the disappearances. His Highest summoning me to his office haunts my dreams. In the dream, guards seize me and bind my hands. His lips are at my ear, telling me my fate, and then The Executor is there with his gun that never misses, the gun that killed my father, my mother, and the parents of all the other Strays. I have nowhere to run. I wake up when the gun goes off, sitting straight up in bed, sweaty and shaking. I won't get any more sleep tonight.

I untangle myself from the sheets, climb out of bed, and turn on the television in the living room. A blonde woman in a white dress suit is smiling as she reports the news. She drones on with stories of His Highest's wonderful traits and all his gracious gifts to the people of Domitus.

"We have breaking news to report to you at this hour. Two families in Science District Three have been taken care of, and our wonderful country is now a safer place. Also, in the news this hour..."

The news anchor continues with some story about a woman who was caught dying her shirts pink, violating the White Laws. She was removed. I can't watch any more. I turn the channel and find an old documentary on Domitus. It's better than the news, so I leave it on, comforted by the sound as I go back to my room. I water the few plants I have on the windowsill. *Stay busy*, I tell myself.

I dress and pull my hair back into a low ponytail. Today is my birthday. I'm twenty and officially an adult. Very briefly, I wonder if the Wexfords will be at my meeting, but quickly dismiss the thought. I haven't seen them since they kicked me out.

I try to eat breakfast, but my stomach is a mess of knots. All I can manage is a glass of water. I put the empty cup in the sink and notice that my hands are shaking. I really need to calm down, but there is the letter on the counter. Just the sight of it has me on the verge of hyperventilation. I glance at the clock on the wall. If I leave now, I will just make it to The Tower on time. I steel myself before opening my door. It will be just fine. Besides, I haven't done anything that would make His Highest suspicious of me. This will be just like any other birthday.

***

When I step outside, the sun is just rising over the houses and shops, momentarily blanching the stones a pale gray. Parked in front of my door is a sleek electro-car with darkly tinted windows. I have never seen one like this before. It's longer than the average electro, and every inch of black metal is polished so that I can see my distorted reflection. A tall man in a crisp white suit gets out of the driver's side and comes around to open the back passenger door for me. I guess His Highest is taking no chances that I'll try to defy him. I slip inside the car, avoiding the gazes of the people passing by.

The driver is silent as he pulls out into the street. We pass buildings full of compliant citizens and shops filled with Domitus-regulated products. A bright red bird darts under the awning of a building; just that flash of color alone makes me feel better.

We pull up to The Tower in minutes. The knots in my stomach intensify. In front of the entrance, two guards wait, guns at their sides. I get out of the car, walk up to them, and state my name. They say nothing and lead me inside. The lobby with its high arches is all black marble. Large urns filled with flowers stand in every corner. A woman sits behind a desk, and one of the guards nods at her as they lead me to an elevator. I hate elevators—hate that there is no escape—but I step inside the little box. An elevator attendant pushes a button that has nothing written next to it. The elevator rushes up without making any stops. I feel nauseated by the time the door opens to reveal a long corridor.

The guards lead me through a series of hallways and then stop in front of two ornate doors made of some kind of wood that I've never seen before. The wood grain alternates between black and dark gray. If I wasn't terrified, I could appreciate the beauty of The Tower. I wipe my sweaty palms on my skirt, worried that His Highest might mistake my nerves for guilt. Still, I can't stop shaking. One of the guards knocks on the door, and I hear a familiar voice say, "Enter."

A guard turns the knob and pushes me inside. I look around for His Highest, but all I can see are the walls of windows that offer a magnificent view of our city. He clears his throat and turns at the sound. He is sitting on a small black couch, watching me, taking in my appearance. I lower my head in respect and wait for him to speak.

"Laura Haywood. How kind of you to come and see me," he says.

His voice is deep and sharp, and his words drip with power. His hair—which should have gone gray by now—is brown and wavy, cropped close to his head. His eyes are a piercing blue, cold and unreadable. He is wearing a charcoal gray suit that looks as if it was made especially for him. In all the years that I have seen him in person, he has never changed.

He gestures to the stiff-looking leather chair across from him. I take a seat and nervously smooth my skirt. He pushes a button in a console on the small table between us and summons tea and sandwiches like this is just a friendly chat between two old friends. He smiles at me when his secretary brings in a tray and places it on the table. She pours him a cup of tea, and His Highest tells me to eat whatever I want. I take a shortbread cookie out of respect, but my stomach is too tangled for me to even nibble at it.

"Well, Laura, I suppose I should say 'happy birthday' though I doubt it is for you."

He pauses to see if I'll disagree, which I won't.

This is always the worst day of the year for me. The Wexfords could have raised me like their own child, maybe even learned to love me, but instead His Highest insisted on reminding them that I was a Stray, as I'm sure he did to all the other Strays. I was nothing but a burden on the regime. We were all burdens. I learned a long time ago to dread my birthday.

"I trust you've been doing well," he continues, sipping his tea. "I was pleased to hear of your graduation from the university. Education is such a noble profession."

He drinks his tea and talks about my life with familiarity. He somehow knows about a crush that I had on Gabriel Nelson, a boy in one of my classes, who laughed at me when I tried to talk to him. What had possessed me to even try, I don't know. I suppose I thought he could see me for who I am after he had been nice enough to help me pick up my books when I'd dropped them.

My face burns with embarrassment. Surely His Highest must know how miserable I am, but my misery only seems to entertain him. He finishes his tea and sets the cup down on the tray. He clears his throat again and uses a napkin to delicately wipe the corners of his mouth.

"So I suppose you've been wondering about this change in our arrangement. There are some things that I believe we need to discuss." His tone has grown serious, and he has my undivided attention. I force my face into an unreadable mask, just like his. "Now that you're an adult, you will be fully responsible for your actions. In the past, I have been lenient of your…indiscretions, but no longer. I will be keeping a much closer eye on all the Strays." A trickle of pure fear runs down my spine. "Do we understand each other, Laura?"

"Yes, Your Highest," I say in a mechanical voice. He smiles at me again, but behind the smile is contempt that he no longer hides from me. My legs tell me to run, but my brain remains in control. To run now would be to condemn myself for sure.

"I believe that is all I have to say. Until next year, Laura." He pushes another button on his console, and the doors open.

Two armed guards escort me to the ground floor. As they are leading me to the front door, I see something out of the corner of my eye: a young man who looks vaguely familiar, hiding behind one of the columns. He sees me notice him and puts his finger to his lips. Before I can even wonder why he is telling me to be quiet, the room seems to erupt.

A man is standing behind the woman at the front desk, a gun pointed at the back of her head. Three more men block the front door. The guards at my sides are just registering that they are under attack. They reach for the guns at their sides, but hesitate when the sounds of several guns cocking echo around the lobby. We are surrounded.

Suddenly, the guard on my left turns his gun on the guard to my right. I see the look of shock as the guard realizes his partner is a traitor. The young man I had first noticed grabs my arm and pulls me toward the back of the lobby.

"It's just not your day, is it, Haywood?" he says.

Before I even have time to register that these men are actually attempting to take over The Tower by force, shots ring around the lobby. Guards start pouring in from every direction, guns already firing. I'm pushed to the floor only seconds before a bullet whizzes right past me. The receptionist, taking in the whole scene in a state of shocked disbelief, is shot through the neck. She collapses back in her chair, blood dying her white clothes a dark red. And then I recognize the young man's face. He's a Stray! I know his name is Max, but I can't remember his last name.

Inch by inch, the rebels work their way farther into the lobby, carrying me with them through the growing pile of dead guards. I realize that they are heading toward a hallway I hadn't noticed before. Most of the rebels block off the entrance as Max, gripping my arm tightly, leads me to the end of the hall. The rebel guard goes to a wall decorated with a large, ornate frame and pushes a panel. A small keyboard appears, and he types in a password. A doorway appears, revealing a stairwell. I try to protest, but the rebel guard and Max pull me up the stairs.

***

The two ornate doors look exactly the same as before. The rebel guard smiles just before he kicks the doors in. A part of me wonders why I have been involved in all this, but before I can consider the possibilities, I see him: The Executor.

He is standing between us and His Highest, a pistol in each hand. His Highest does not seem the least bit worried that there are rebels who have made it as far as his own office. He is reclining exactly where I left him only a few minutes before.

"Laura, I'm impressed. I would never have guessed that you were involved in this coup the entire time you were in my office," he says.

The blood drains from my face.

"She had nothing to do with this," Max says beside me.

The Executor looks back at His Highest, but His Highest shakes his head. I realize that he is waiting for the command to kill.

"Ah, Max," His Highest says, "I must say that I didn't expect you to get this far." Max and the guard exchange uneasy looks. "Yes, I knew you were up to something. I always know. I won't say that I'm sorry you've involved Miss Haywood. It will be much easier to get rid of all the Strays now. It's just a shame that you all turned out so terribly. You could have been a real asset to the regime."

"You killed our parents," Max says.

"I gave you new ones, better ones."

"And they hated every minute we were around."

His Highest shrugs. The Executor glares at all of us, waiting for his signal. Visions of all the public executions I had been forced to watch over the years run through my head. I cannot believe that I'm actually standing in the same room with him. His Highest taps his fingers on the table. The Executor opens fire, and my vision goes black.

***

Voices all talk at once, making it difficult to understand anything being said.

"When do you think she'll wake up?" says a female voice near my head. "You're sure she isn't shot? There's a lot of blood here."

"I'm sure. She just fainted."

I open my eyes a fraction and see his face directly over mine. He smiles.

"Hi, Laura. You're all right," he adds when he sees that I'm about to panic. "I guess I don't need to introduce myself."

I shake my head. I remember seeing him when we were children playing at a small park. Mrs. Wexford had seen us talking and yanked me away. She said, "Stay away from Max Anderson. His father was no good, and I'll wager he's no better."

I haven't seen him very often over the years. There aren't that many Strays in the country—most of us live in the city—but a few were taken to some of the districts farther outside the city. Looking at Max now, a part of me thinks that Mrs. Wexford may have been right. His clothes are torn and stained with blood. His nose is crooked like it's been broken before. He looks wild.

He helps me sit up, and my vision sways for a moment. When I'm certain that I'm not going to throw up, I look around the room, trying to figure out where I am. I'm in a seemingly ordinary living room. I've been lying on an ugly plaid couch covered in dog hair, though I don't see a dog anywhere. Everything else in the room is equally ratty—piles of pizza boxes take up a corner, and a layer of dust coats everything. There is not a single picture in the room to give me a clue as to whose house I'm in, but I'm getting the feeling that no one actually lives here. Everything looks old and worn, as if this house was abandoned a long time ago.

"What happened?" I asked. "We were in The Tower. His Highest—"

"Is dead, Laura," Max says.

I look around at the other people in the room and see the truth of this statement reflected in their pleased expressions. There are only five people in the room, so I wonder if all the other rebels in The Tower were killed. I notice the rebel guard isn't among us. I try to remember what happened after His Highest tapped on the table, but my memory is blank.

"Please tell me what happened."

Max gestures to one of the other guys in the room, and he hands me a glass of water. The glass doesn't look very clean, but I'm thirsty and gulp it down anyways.

"We've been planning this for a long time. Some of the other Strays and I decided a while back that His Highest had to come down. So we started trying to figure out how to get into The Tower."

"But what happened in that office? How did we get out of there alive?" I see a few of the other guys in the room look at each other uncomfortably.

"It all happened really fast. The Executor started shooting. I barely had time to get you out of the way, but I shot him. I shot His Highest. I put a bullet in his forehead, Laura. He's dead."

It takes me a minute to absorb this. His Highest is dead. The man who has made my life hell, who had my parents killed, who killed hundreds over the years, is dead. And then I remembered the other man who was in that room, equally if not more dangerous.

"What happened to The Executor?"

"We were all shooting at each other, and when His Highest was dead, I ran. I picked you up and ran. I didn't look back."

"So he could still be alive?" I ask. Max's eyes tell me all I need to know.

"The last time I saw him, he had been shot, but was still very much alive."

I jump off the couch. I need to get out of here, away from these people. What have they gotten me involved in? The ground begins to shake. I look at everyone else, but they're looking out the window at the city skyline in the distance. The shaking rumbles to a stop.

It is eerily quiet, quieter than I have ever heard. Suddenly sound comes from every direction—like screaming or laughing, or maybe both.

"Welcome to the revolution, Laura," Max says.

I walk to the window. The others step aside so that I can see what has happened. The streets are full of people; they are crying, screaming, and some are cheering. Far in the distance is a gaping hole where

The Tower used to stand. Smoke billows up into the sky, mixing with the clouds.

"We decided it would be best if that building was gone. It represents...well, represented, His Highest's power," says one of the men by the window. Some of the others nod in agreement, but they are strangely silent as we all watch the smoke.

"But The Executor is still alive," I remind them.

"Maybe. Even if he is, we'll get him, too," Max says, placing a hand on my shoulder.

"Why me? Why get me involved?" I ask, but a part of me already knows the answer.

"We're Strays, Laura. We need to stick together."

His Highest made a mistake when he constantly reminded us of who we were, of where we came from. He never gave the Wexfords a chance to learn to love me, and I'm certain that the other Strays had the same upbringing as me. His Highest made many mistakes over the years, but we were his biggest. The corners of my mouth turn up as I look into Max's eyes. His Highest made a mistake.

BISHOP FARM

A loud snap and a strange rattle woke me. I huddled under my covers, trying to place the foreign sounds, when I heard my door open.

"Molly, get up. We have to go," Dad said from my darkened doorway, his silhouette barely visible in the dim morning light.

"What's going on? What's that sound?"

"Just get your clothes and come downstairs, now. We're going to the cabin."

Another burst echoed in the distance, and I realized that the moment I had been dreading for weeks had finally come. The protests and riots that had started the month before must have escalated overnight. The sound was my worst nightmare: gunfire.

I threw my covers back, ran to my closet, and grabbed my duffel bag from the top shelf. I stuffed everything that my hands touched into the bag— jeans, T-shirts, underwear. When it could hold no more, I forced the zipper closed. I pulled on my favorite pair of jeans and a dark shirt and shoved my feet into my hiking boots. I forced my arms through the sleeves of my coat. Virginia might not be chilly right now, but the mountains of West Virginia would be. I dragged my bag down the hallway toward the living room, noticing that many of the pictures on the walls had been removed. My parents must have been up for hours preparing for our departure.

None of the lights were on in the house, but I could see my dad in the kitchen packing cans into boxes. My mom was in Devin's room, talking to him in a soothing voice as she helped him pack his clothes. She led him into the kitchen and told him to sit at the table while we packed the car.

My mom and dad loaded up our beat-up minivan, moving as quietly as they could from the driveway to the house and back again. Every time the door opened, the sounds of gunfire and shouts grew louder. I tried to keep my fear to myself, for Devin's sake. I wondered how close the mobs of rioters were from our house.

After the last bag was loaded into the van, Dad came back inside and looked at the clock on the wall.

"You have thirty minutes to say goodbye to whoever you need to, but don't leave the neighborhood. Do you understand me, Molly?"

I nodded, my heart pounding in my chest. "Are you sure it's safe?"

"It's still a few miles away from here, and the neighborhood seems pretty quiet. I have to go do something; I'll be back in thirty minutes. You have that long to say your goodbyes. Do not leave the neighborhood. Do you understand? And if you see anything at all, you come straight back here."

He leaned forward and kissed my forehead. My mom hugged him tightly, and I turned my face away. Devin's eyes were wide, and he was trying to hold onto my mom's pant leg as if afraid she would leave him behind. Dad pulled himself away from us and went back outside. I didn't hear the engine start. I realized that wherever he was going, it was close enough that he could walk.

A minute later I eased out the back door and took off running. My feet guided me through the grey light by memory. I pulled my cell phone from my pocket and slowed down only long enough to call my boyfriend, Thomas. Voicemail. I cursed and tried my best friend, Angela. It went straight to voicemail, too. Starting to panic, I dialed Thomas's number a second time. Voicemail, again. I tried a third time only to get the same result. It was all right, though. I knew where I was going. I cut through a backyard, knocking over a garden gnome in the process. At the end of the block I turned right and ran as fast as I could until the road ended at a dirt driveway, nearly hidden from the overgrowth of trees and weeds.

The driveway ended in front of the old Milton Plantation. The Victorian-style house was on the verge of falling down, the remnants of the Antebellum South slowly crumbling into obscurity. Wisteria grew up the side and had broken through the windows of the first floor. One day, the house would be reclaimed by the land. It was beautiful. Thomas had told me about the place, and I'd always wondered how I could have lived so close to it my whole life and never known of its existence. It was Thomas who had suggested that we use it as our secret spot.

When I'd started dating Thomas, my dad had objected. Thomas wasn't what my dad wanted for me. He played guitar, didn't eat meat, and regularly took in stray animals. Dad was always telling me that I needed to find someone who could take care of me, someone strong. I'd never really understood what he'd meant by that. To me, Thomas was perfect. He listened when I talked and cared about how I felt.

I expertly navigated the rotting stairs of the wraparound porch, pulled open the heavy front door, and yelled his name over the sound of the creaking hinges. I waited in the foyer, but there was no reply.

"Thomas! Oh God, where are you?" My voice echoed through the room.

I went to the back of the house, passing the staircase that had collapsed years ago. The sleeping bag was still rolled up in the corner; the candles were scattered around the small bedroom, but none had been lit recently. I sank to my knees, shaking with the realization that I might never see him again.

This was not how I had imagined my senior year. I had pictured us graduating together, maybe going to college at the same school. I had even imagined marrying him one day. The country collapsing had not been in my plan.

Just as I was about to leave, I noticed Thomas's sketchpad in the corner, his pencil case lying on top of it. I opened the pad and flipped past the drawings of me, each one more detailed than the last. I saw myself lying on the sleeping bag, my eyes half closed and a coy smile on my lips. I made myself turn to a blank page, take out one of the pencils, and write.

I told him where we were going and how to get to the cabin in West Virginia. I gave him every road he could take if the interstate was blocked. I begged him to find me. I promised him I would wait for him. Then I left the letter in the metal mailbox that still hung by the front door. We always left notes for each other there, and I knew that if he came here, he would find it.

I made my way home, calling his cell phone over and over again, but none of the calls would go through. Just as I was walking up to the backdoor of my house, an old truck rattled into the driveway, the sound of the muffler joining the distant sound of gunfire. My dad hopped out of the back of the truck and jogged to the house.

"Joel is coming with us. Come on, let's get going."

I climbed into the backseat of the minivan and held Devin's trembling hand as we pulled out of the neighborhood. Joel's truck followed behind us. My mom told Devin to close his eyes when we got onto the highway. A body was sprawled on the ground—a man—with a pool of blood spreading out around him. No one said anything until we left the suburbs behind us.

"It'll take us a little longer to get to West Virginia this way, but we'll make it. I promise," Dad said.

I leaned my head against the backseat and watched the sun rise over the fields that flew past my window. As we drove deeper into the rural counties of Virginia, it seemed surreal to think that behind us the country was falling apart. My dad turned on the radio and listened to the news reports until my mom asked him to turn it off. Instead, he just turned the volume down until it was only a murmur.

***

"What do you miss most from before, Molly?" Devin asked me as he pulled feathers from a dead chicken and shoved them into a bag. Nothing would be wasted; even the feathers would be used to stuff pillows.

"I miss going to the mall," I told him. "I miss watching TV."

"I miss skateboarding and my Nintendo and my friends," he said, naming the same things he'd named the last time he had asked me.

This was a game we played almost every day, going over all the things we missed from before the country was plunged into chaos. I didn't tell him that I hated this game. It only reminded me of all the things we no longer had, but for Devin it was a way to remember. He was only ten, and every day that passed separated him from his memories of our old life.

Our family was lucky, luckier than most. My dad had definitely seen it coming. Unemployment had risen to epic proportions; stocks were falling rapidly while the price of food went up. There had been signs, and when my dad was laid off almost a year before it finally happened, he started spending more and more time at our cabin. He installed solar panels on the roof and fixed up the neglected rooms inside. Then he filled the basement with boxes full of toilet paper and built shelves to hold cans of beans and soup. He bought five-gallon buckets full of oatmeal and fifty-pound sacks of rice, sugar, and flour. He said it didn't really matter how much money we spent preparing the cabin because in the end it would save us. He was right.

The cabin was only a few hours from our home, though now it felt like home was an eternity away. The nearest town was over thirty minutes away, and the national forest lay just over the next ridge. It was as isolated as we could ever hope to be—our own private mountain oasis. He called it Bishop Farm, after his mother's family who had bought the land over a hundred years ago. We had spent a lot of time there as children, hiking up the mountain and fishing in the river that split the mountain in half. Every now and then we had close encounters with bears or hikers who had strayed from the trails in the national forest, but our family had always felt safest—and closest—when we were on our mountain. During the first few weeks, there had been shots and what sounded like large explosions a few miles from the farm. My dad had spent a lot of that time up in one of the watch towers he'd set up around the perimeter. He said he never saw anything, but sometimes I think he just said that so we'd feel better.

Dad had put a lot of effort into shaping the cabin, and the mountain it sat on, into a fortress. He spent hours building a fence around the entire property, six-feet high and topped with sharp barbed wire. *To keep people out*, he'd said. My mom had rolled her eyes through most of this, but she had let him have his way in the hopes that it would keep him busy. She had her job as a nurse, and as long as she was working we were okay. I realized later that my mom had tried very hard to hide her worry for my dad. Now, though, she was grateful.

"You missed a spot," I said to Devin, pointing to a clump of feathers underneath the bird's wing. In my lap was a bowl of green beans, beside me another bowl where I tossed the ends of the beans as I snapped each one.

The farm had done well this year—much better than last year—and I grudgingly had to admit that it was because Joel was here. But Joel had brought his wife and daughter, too. I heard my parents arguing about them once, when they thought I couldn't hear. Mom had never cared for Joel—even before we were all forced to live together—but Dad made a better argument, and in the end he'd won. They were extra mouths, but they were also extra hands. Together we could all tend to the garden and small greenhouse. We took care of the chickens and the two dairy cows that my dad had bought only a month before the collapse. Joel was a few years older than my dad, and he knew his way around a farm.

His wife, Ms. Shannon, was quiet, always staying near the house to do the wash or help my mom cook dinner. Not Heather, though. She was just an extra mouth.

I looked up from my bowl to check on Devin again and spotted Heather walking towards us, her thumbs hooked into the pockets of her cut-off denim shorts. Her oversized flannel shirt was tied up under her breasts so that her stomach was visible. She wore large round sunglasses like she was going to the beach, but I knew she wore them so no one would be able to see she had no eye makeup on. She kept her hair in two braids on either side of her face to hide her split ends, as if any of us really cared that she didn't look perfect. I looked down at my hands and saw the calluses I had painstakingly earned, and smiled.

Heather sat on a tree stump near my chair, her legs crossed as one foot bobbed up and down. She was nothing like her mom. I liked Ms. Shannon. She'd easily accepted the changes in our circumstances. Ms. Shannon looked at me when we talked and she always had a smile for me, even when life on the mountain felt like a prison sentence. I looked at Heather and wondered why she wasn't more like her mom. I knew that I was more serious than my own mother, not as quick to laugh, but I always liked to think that I was growing into a woman my mom could be proud of. Looking at Heather, I couldn't help but feel sorry for Ms. Shannon.

"What have you done today, Heather?" I asked, making no attempt to disguise dislike for her. After almost two years of being trapped with her I was tired of trying to be nice.

"You don't have to harass me, Molly. I already got shit from my dad this morning." She examined her fingernails as she spoke. "And then Mom made me wash clothes with her for like a fucking hour. It was awful."

I gave her a look and pointed my head in Devin's direction. Through the lenses of her sunglasses I saw her roll her eyes at me. The urge to punch her was overwhelming. She knew that she wasn't supposed to cuss in front of him, but she did it anyways.

"I have a secret. Do you wanna hear?" Heather asked as she twirled the end of one braid around her finger.

I dropped the green bean I was snapping, set the bowl aside, and wiped my hands. Heather smirked, and I could almost feel the smugness radiating from her.

"Hey, Devin, you're just about done. Why don't you go inside and see if Mom needs help with anything."

He let out a whoop and dropped the now nude chicken into a tall, stainless-steel pot. I waited until he was almost to the house before I spoke.

"What is it this time?" I asked. It was not the first time Heather had taunted me with secrets that turned out to be nothing at all.

Heather shrugged her shoulder and continued to look at her nails. I threw a green bean at her, and she finally looked at me. She looked so bored that for a moment I almost felt sorry for her. And then she rolled her eyes again.

"Let's just say that it has to do with your daddy and my daddy."

She giggled a little, and the urge to smack her flared up in me again. I waited a moment to see if she would give up her secret, but she just continued to smile at me. A strange sensation crawled up my spine and the thought that perhaps this time she was being serious flashed through my mind. She really did know something.

"Fine," I said, "if you aren't going to tell me, then I'll just have to go find out for myself."

I covered the bowl of snapped beans with a cloth and got up. If there was something going on, then I wanted to know what it was.

"They won't want you getting in the way," she called after me, but I wasn't stopping.

My dad had changed in the last two years. His dark hair had become peppered with gray, his face more lined. The happy expression in his eyes had been replaced with a look of cold-hearted determination. He was a man obsessed with trying to keep us all safe and alive. He was no longer the kind-hearted man who had put bandages on my skinned knees or planted kisses on my forehead. I couldn't even remember the last time he had given me a hug.

My boots crunched through the freshly fallen leaves, and in the silence of the outdoors, the sound seemed to echo all around me. Any attempts to walk quietly were futile. Just as I was approaching the barn my dad came out, his shotgun resting on his hip. The sight of it made me stop mid-stride, but he had seen me, and I had no choice but to keep walking.

"What's going on?" I asked.

"Nothing for you to worry about."

"Something is going on, and I want to know what it is." I tried to keep my voice steady. From inside the barn I heard a muffled scream. "You have someone in there."

"Turn yourself around and go inside. This doesn't concern you."

I wasn't giving up. I kept my eyes on his when I demanded to know who it was. He glared at me for a minute. My heart was pounding in my chest with a mixture of fear and excitement.

"It's Thomas," he said, and my heart dropped. With his free hand he reached up and pointed at me, a familiar gesture that usually meant I had done something wrong. Then he leaned in close to me, so close that I could see the specks of blood on the stubble of his chin. "I sure would like to know how he found his way here, Molly."

I had finally begun to believe that I would never see him again. When the first few days turned into weeks and then months, my tears dried. Something must have happened to him. It had to be the only reason that he had never come for me, and now just hearing his name nearly took my breath away. I had to keep my emotions under control. I had toughened up a lot since the collapse, and no matter how much

I wanted to cry and yell at my dad, I couldn't do that.

"Have you hurt him?" I asked Dad, trying to keep my voice steady.

"Not much," he finally told me.

"Can I see him?"

Dad thought about it for a minute, eyeing me the whole time, before opening the door to the barn and calling for Joel. Joel came out, wiping his hands on an old dirty rag. He had blood and scrapes on his knuckles. I had to hold back all my emotions. I needed to keep my head clear, to find a way to talk Dad and Joel into letting Thomas stay.

I stepped into the dim barn and closed the door behind me. I could see him clearly in the beam of light that shone down from the loft above. He was tied to a chair. One eye was nearly swollen shut, and his nose looked broken. His hair was matted with blood and straw. He lifted his head, swaying slightly.

"Molly?"

I almost fell as I ran to him. I pulled the ropes that bound his hands to the back of the chair, and he slumped forward into my arms.

"Oh God, Thomas."

"I'm okay," he said, but his voice sounded weak.

I wrapped my arms around him, rejoicing in the familiar feel of his body. He was thinner, maybe even more muscular. His brown hair had been cut short with a dull pair of scissors, and his face was much tanner than before, but still, he looked the same to me.

"I thought I'd never see you again. It's been almost two years, Thomas. Where have you been?"

He winced as I used the edge of my shirt to wipe some of the blood from his face.

"I found your letter probably less than an hour after you'd left it, but it was too late. You had already gone."

He was quiet while I poured him a cup of water from the jug my dad always kept by the door. I watched him take a few sips. His breathing was raspy as he struggled to swallow. Looking at him, I kept expecting to wake from a dream and discover that none of this—Thomas's arrival, our life in the mountains, the collapse of all I'd ever known—none of it had ever happened, but as the beam of sunshine illuminated his battered face, I had to acknowledge that this was all very real.

"I'm glad you got away. If you had waited any longer, you might not have made it." He rubbed his wrists where the ropes had burned his skin.

"What happened? Was it really bad?"

"The military showed up the day after you left. They tried to stop all the looters, but they only made things worse. Me and my mom hid in our house for over a week, praying that things would calm down before we ran out of food, but they didn't."

He stopped to catch his breath as if every word was painful, but I didn't want him to stop talking to me. I could have listened to him all day. I had forgotten how much I loved the subtle rasp of his voice, as if he was a smoker even though he'd never smoked a cigarette in his life.

"I had to go out there, to try and find food for us." He paused again, and a strange look came into his eyes.

"Molly, I'm not the same person I used to be. The things I saw, Molly. The things I had to do—"

"Shhh, it's okay. I know."

I wasn't stupid. I knew that there was the possibility that Thomas had done things he might not be proud of just to survive, but still he was here. It was enough for me.

"Thomas, where's your mom? Why isn't she with you?"

"She's gone," he said.

From the look in his eyes I could tell that he didn't want to talk about it. He tried to stand only to sway unsteadily. I caught him and guided him back to the chair.

"Look, I'll leave, and I'll promise your dad that I won't tell anyone about this place. I just had to see you. I had to know you were okay."

"No. I'm not losing you again. Besides," I pulled pieces of straw from his hair, "now that you're here, Dad has to let you stay."

A knock came from outside, and before I could respond my mom came through the door. She said nothing. She took Thomas's arm and led him out of the barn. I followed them to the house. My dad and Joel watched my mom half carry Thomas. Before I could back out, I turned and started walking towards them. I heard my mom say something to me, but I ignored her and kept walking. Joel saw me coming, but Dad's eyes never left Thomas; his shotgun rested on his hip.

"Can I speak to you? Alone?" I asked my dad.

His steely gaze finally turned to me.

Dad nodded to Joel, who headed off in the direction of the greenhouse. I waited until he was gone before I spoke.

"I know you're mad," I started.

"You have no idea how I feel, Molly."

There was so much in his face, so many hidden emotions that he was not willing to talk about. I nervously pulled at a loose thread on my jacket. I wasn't sure if I wanted to have this talk with him yet, but I couldn't put it off either. The muffled cry I'd heard that night still echoed in my ears. I felt sick just thinking about what my dad could do to Thomas, and I may never have known if it hadn't been for Heather. I closed my eyes and took a deep breath to steady myself. When I was certain that I could talk without showing fear, I opened my eyes and met my dad's gaze.

"Dad, I know you're also scared. I know you worry about all of us. With the planning for winter and next spring, it's no wonder you're worried, but you're not alone. We all worry." His eyes were like steel, cold and impenetrable. "You have to understand, though, that I trust Thomas as much as I trust you. I love him, and when we were leaving, he was the only person that I couldn't bear to live without. Please, Dad, you have to let him stay."

He finally set his shotgun down and leaned it against a tree stump. He turned to the fence and rested his arms along the top. One of the cows pulled at the grass nearby and occasionally lifted its head to moo at the other cow.

"You know it's not that easy, Molly. For all we know, your Thomas has joined some kind of gang and they're sittin' out there right now waiting for a signal to attack us. As long as we have food and shelter and a fresh supply of water, then we're vulnerable."

I understood—I did—but there was just no way that I was going to send Thomas back out into the wilderness when we had no way of knowing that he would survive. Every night we turned on the old radio and went through the stations, waiting for a voice to break through the static. Occasionally we picked up someone reporting, but in two years there'd been very little good news. We were on our own; there was no government riding in on a white horse to save us. If Thomas went out there again, I would certainly lose him forever, but in the back of my mind I also had to admit to myself that my dad and Joel would never let him leave. Just two years before I never would have thought that my dad was capable of killing anyone, but I couldn't be certain anymore. I had to find a different way to make him see reason.

"Dad," I said as I weighed my words, "you have to be realistic, though. How long do you expect this to last? Forever? What happens when Devin grows up? What happens when I want to get married or start a family? I know things are different now," I added quickly, seeing the look that he was giving me, "but that doesn't change what I want for my life. For all we know, things could get better one day, and we'll be able to go home."

Dad turned around and leaned his back up against the fence. His eyes drifted to the mountains in the distance; the fall leaves created a kaleidoscope of colors all blending together in a breathtaking view. I doubted that he saw the beauty around us. His eyes were constantly looking for threats.

"I know you expected to have your own life one day, Molly, but right now we have to live day by day. If I lost you," he said, his voice cracking, "or your mother, or Devin, I would never be able to live with myself."

"I know, Dad, but if you send Thomas away, then you've already lost me."

His eyes snapped back to mine. It was the harshest thing I had ever said to him. Even in the beginning of our life here I had never taken my anger out on him. Devin had screamed and yelled at him for weeks, but not me. I had tried to always be strong, even if I was screaming on the inside. Dad pushed off the fence and used the toe of his boot to dislodge a rock from the soil.

"So it's like that, is it? You sure aren't making this easy for me."

I could see fear in his eyes for the first time in a long time. He was quiet, his eyes never leaving mine.

"I guess I never realized you were that serious about him."

"It is. I am. I've grown up a lot in the last two years, but that doesn't mean I stopped thinking about Thomas," I told him. I tugged at my jacket again, wishing that I didn't have to have this talk with my dad. I don't know what I imagined would happen when I finally brought a guy home and announced we were getting married or moving in together, but I know that I had never imagined telling my dad I was in love quite like this. Heather came around the side of the house. She stopped and watched us, probably curious about Thomas. Dad noticed her, too.

"That girl is irritating as hell," he said. His arm came around my shoulders and he pulled me into his chest. He rested his chin on the top of my head. I wrapped my arms around him, and for a moment, it felt like I was still his little girl and everything that had happened was still far in my future. The tension in the air dissipated.

"Thanks, Dad."

He let out a loud sigh but it ended in a laugh. We started walking back toward the house, and I noticed my dad's eyes do another quick scan of the tree line. I wondered if there would ever be anyone in the barn again, if my dad had maybe changed a little after today.

"Molly, it's Thomas! He's here!" Devin ran out of the house, the screen door slamming behind him.

"I know, little man," I said. "Where is he?"

He opened the door and tore through the house. Mom had Thomas lying on the couch with a cold compress over his eye. Ms. Shannon was in the kitchen, and the smells of dinner were already beginning to seep into the living room. Mom and

Dad exchanged a look, but Mom smiled, so I had to assume that she understood Thomas was staying.

I sat down beside him and took his hand in mine. He was half asleep, his head beginning to fall back against the couch. I couldn't even begin to imagine what he had gone through to get here, but I was glad he had made it.

Heather slinked into the living room and plopped into a chair. She eyed my hand holding tight to Thomas's. I waited for her to say something, to make a remark about how unfair all of this was for her. I suddenly realized that I was in her debt. Maybe I could be nicer to her. Maybe she really just needed a friend all this time. She got up and went into the kitchen. I heard her ask her mom if she needed help, and then her mother's surprised response. Maybe she wouldn't be so bad anymore.

Devin danced around the living room until my mom finally told him to go outside and get the green beans I'd left. Through the window I could see Joel chopping wood, splitting each log in one graceful motion with the axe. Every now and then he stopped, pulled his rag from his pocket, and wiped his forehead. I watched the woodpile grow as I held Thomas' hand. In the corner of my eye, I saw my mom lean up to kiss my dad's cheek. I closed my eyes and breathed a sigh of relief.

ABOUT THE AUTHOR

Kristina Turnage discovered her love of stories at a young age, reading every book she could get her hands on until she realized that she could write her own. She completed her BA in English, concentrating in Creative Writing, at North Carolina State University in 2013. She now lives with her husband and their dog in Raleigh.